Frogs Do Not Like Dragons

Patricia Forde and Joëlle Dreidemy

For my parents, Tommy and Detta Forde,
with all my love.
P.F.

To Fabrice, the magic cat, who
managed to transform a little frog called
David into a charming prince.
J.D.

EGMONT

We bring stories to life

Book Band: Turquoise

First published in Great Britain 2010
This Reading Ladder edition published 2016
by Egmont UK Limited
The Yellow Building, 1 Nicholas Road, London W11 4AN
Text copyright © Patricia Forde 2010
Illustrations copyright © Joëlle Dreidemy 2010
The author and illustrator have asserted their moral rights
ISBN 978 1 4052 8206 2
www.egmont.co.uk
A CIP catalogue record for this title is available from the British Library.
Printed in Singapore
46577/5

Series consultant: Nikki Gamble

Frogs Do Not Like Dragons

Reading Ladder

Frogs do not like dragons. I discovered that the day my sister Lola got locked in the bathroom.

Nan was taking care of us but she wasn't much help.

LOLA?

Luckily, I am very good at coming up with ideas.

6

'Lola!' I said. 'Just turn the key and –'

'I can't reach the key,' Lola said crossly.

'I am only five and three quarters, you know.'

'Don't be silly,' I said. 'You could reach it before. How else did you lock yourself in?'

Silence.

'I did not lock this door, Natalie
Nugent,' Lola said softly. 'Rubella
the witch locked this door, and now
I'm her prisoner.'

Just then, Mum and Dad arrived home.
'Come along, darling! Open the door
for Mummy!'

Uh-oh.

'Dotty Duck is on television!' Dad said.
'Be a good little girl and come out of
the bathroom.'

'I can't come out, Mummy,' Lola said.
'Rubella the witch has locked me in,
and she's standing in front of the door
with the key in her pocket.'

My father called the fire brigade.

'Do you think you could stand on the
toilet and open the window?' the fire
chief asked Lola.

'I don't think that would be a good idea,' Lola said. 'The window is high, and I'm only five and three quarters. I might fall and hurt the dragon.'

'Dragon?' said the fire chief.

'Yes,' said Lola. 'There's a scaly, green dragon in here with Rubella the witch and me. I think he's asleep, and I

wouldn't want to wake him. His name
is Fizz. *Fizz!* Isn't that a lovely name
for a dragon?'

Mum had another go.

'Lola, my love! Do you think you
could take the key and slide it under

the door? I'm sure that cross old witch wouldn't mind.'

Me? Cross?

Silence.

'Lola?' said Mum again.

'I wish you hadn't called her a cross old witch,' said Lola at last. 'She didn't like it, and now she's cast a spell.

The bathroom is filling up with frogs, which is not good, because frogs do not like dragons.'

'Now, Lola . . .' Dad began, but Lola
was still talking.

'Oh dear! The frogs have really

annoyed Fizz now. His skin has turned
blue and his eyes are very red. I do
hope he's not a fire-blowing dragon!'

'Don't worry about the fire. We can deal with fire,' said the fire chief. 'It's the witch and the dragon that might give us some trouble.'

My father called the police.

'Well, well!' said the first policeman.

'What seems to be the trouble?'

'No trouble at all,' said the fire chief.

'We have everything under control.'

'No, you don't!' said my mother.
'My daughter is locked in the bathroom,
and you have no idea
how to deal with
witches or dragons!'

Ooops!

The fire chief's
face turned red.

'Now listen, little girl,' said the second
policeman. 'Open the door immediately
and come out with your hands up!'

'I'm sorry, Mr Policeman,' Lola said, 'but I can't do that. You see, Rubella the witch has a nasty cat with one eye

and three legs. The cat is chasing the frogs. Fizz the dragon is furious, and is blowing fire all over the place. I have to turn the taps on or the house might burn down.'

'No!' cried Dad.
'Do not turn on the taps!'
It was too late. I could
hear water gushing. My
father called the plumber.

NOW! You need
to come now!

The corridor outside the bathroom was now full of people. Luckily, just then, I had another great idea.

'Excuse me,' I said, but no one was listening.

'I am in charge here,' said the plumber.
'This is a bathroom. Plumbers and
bathrooms go together.'

'No, you're not in charge!' said the policeman. 'I was here before you!'

'A dragon is blowing fire,' said the fire chief. 'That means that I'm in charge!'

In the bathroom, the water suddenly stopped flowing. I pushed my way forward and whispered into the keyhole. 'Lola!'

My sister sighed on the other side of
the door.

'Yes? What is it now?' she asked.

'We need to talk!' I said.

'Well, hurry,' said Lola. 'I'm rather busy in here. The frogs are in a panic, trying to escape from the witch's cat, and they've blocked the plughole.

GULP!

This is very bad news, because I had to run the taps when the frogs upset Fizz. Now the water is filling up the bathroom and I don't think Rubella is able to swim . . .'

'Nan baked an apple pie,' I managed to say when she stopped to take a breath.

Silence.

Everybody waited.

'So?' said Lola. 'It's only apple pie . . .'

'Yes,' I agreed. 'Only apple pie with a crisp, buttery crust and soft yellow apples swimming in luscious, sweet juice. Mmmm . . .'

Lola said nothing.

Then, I thought I heard a scuffle. Was
the bathroom window opening?
The fire chief spoke.
'You could always ask the witch to
leave and take her cat with her,' he
said. 'The frogs aren't a problem. We
can deal with frogs.'

The policeman nodded in agreement. Then he shook himself and scowled at the fire chief. With that, the plumber stamped his foot. 'Frogs are bad news in a bathroom,' he said.

The policeman cleared his throat. 'Perhaps the zoo would make a home for the dragon,' he said. 'We could help deliver him and . . .'

Cccrrrkkk! The key scraped in the lock.
Slowly, the door opened. Lola stood
before us, calm and unruffled.

'Don't be silly,' she said to the policeman. 'Dragons don't live in zoos. You should know that! After all, you are a policeman. Now, where's my apple pie?'

I went into the bathroom. Nothing.
Nothing unusual, that is.
No witch. No dragon. No cat with
one eye and three legs.

Then, I saw something twitch in the bath. A fat, green frog was struggling to squeeze through the plughole.

All about him was dragon dust, sparkling in the sunlight. Every time the frog looked at it, his whole body shivered and his eyes widened in horror. And that is how I discovered that . . .

Frogs Do Not Like Dragons